MW01199909

WET DREAM

A PARANORMAL INTERRACIAL EROTIC ROMANCE

LEXI ESME

WET DREAM

by Lexi Esme

.Contents

CHAPTER ONE

"Did you make a purchase from the lingerie store yester-day?"

The question is almost stupid. I already have the bank statement in hand, but perhaps I wish he would at least have the decency to come clean with it or to tell me something that would make all of this better. Something or anything that would make it so that I didn't just waste all this time for nothing.

Jerome, the man I've wasted a year of my life on sits on my beat-up couch, laid back with his feet outstretched on the coffee table beside the X-Box I'd bought him for Christmas last year—each day I regret buying it for him more and more.

And now, my eyes settle on the couch beneath him; when I bought it, it was cream white and now it's nothing but a shade of mustard yellow from all the stains. I tried to have it deep cleaned, but it always ends up turning back into a mess, so I gave up. Now, I'm starting to understand that it wasn't cleaning all the messes that I should have given up on.

I should have given up on him.

"What the hell are you talking about?" He grunts, eyes not even leaving the videogame on the TV screen as he takes a drag from his blunt and then a sip from his beer.

"I'm talking about the call I just got from the bank that all of my goddamn money is gone. Purchases on beer, lingerie, and a lot of cash withdrawals that don't make any sense to me" I toss the bank statement in his direction.

"If you're going to buy your whores gifts at least don't use my fucking money!"

Now that seems to grab his attention.

He places the beer bottle on the coffee table as he turns to face me. The look of anger on his face used to scare the living daylights out of me, but now I feel nothing but remorse.

"YOUR goddamn money? Last time I checked, it's a *joint* account meaning whatever is in there is mine too."

"You're right. It is a joint account but the last time I *also* checked I was the only one in this house that's been putting money in it. I mean when was the last time you even got up from that couch?" I ask, already knowing what he would answer back, so I beat him to the punch.

"-And no, playing basketball with your friends doesn't count because you shouldn't even be hanging out with them! Not when you're barely getting by. Did you even go to that interview I set up for you?"

"Damn! When did you become such a bitch, Deonne!? You're worse than my goddamn mother. If I had known that this is what you would be like, I would never have even moved in!" he lets out a breath of exasperation.

His statement feels like the final nail in the coffin. After all this time, after all I've given, and after all he's taken, he can't even have the decency to be sorry about it. All the hesitation I've been carrying for so long dissipates. This has been a long time coming, I was just too blind to see it.

My fists unclench, I didn't even realize that I was holding on so tightly. Letting out a deep breath, a moment of clarity hits me. I didn't even notice I was in a haze for so long.

"Then why did you even move in with me?" My voice comes out as barely a whisper, and that seems to hit him. I see his features soften.

"Because I love you, Deonne. I'm sorry. I know I made some mistakes, but I'm trying. You know it's been hard out here after my boss fired me for no reason–"

That wasn't true...he was fired after going into work late numerous times, and that was if he went at all. When I snap back to focus, it's to catch the end of his spiel:

"--Sure I hit a rough patch, but doesn't everyone? I'm trying! You have to believe me when I say I am trying." He stands up and walks toward me. He grabs my shoulders and Jerome looks at me with the same face that would usually have me crawling back to him. His sad brown eyes always had an effect on me, but this time, they just didn't.

I'm too fed up. Shrugging out of his hold, I step back and wrap my arms around myself.

"I don't, Jerome. I don't believe you even as much as I want to. I just can't anymore."

His face changes way too quickly, and the soft expression of remorse and guilt distorts into rage. He grabs the beer bottle, throwing it across the room and it smashes against the wall before falling to the floor in a plethora of broken green shards.

I flinch at the sound as he stomps closer to me, each step he takes I take one back until my back is pressed against the door. He's never hit me- for all the bullshit he put me through that's one thing he never did but with his fists clenched so tightly and his nostrils flaring, I think that he just might.

But I'm not scared. He's taken too much from me.

"What? You think you can just throw me the hell out!? I'm all you have Deonne!" He slams his fist against the wall beside my head. "When everyone leaves you. I'll be the one who's here.

I'm it, Deonne. You're not going to get anything better than this. Who else would want you—when you're a four at best? If you don't have me, you're gonna die alone. If you don't have me, you'll have nothing!"

His words hit me like a truck because a part of me actually believes him. That's why I stayed so long, but now anything, even if it is nothing, is better than this.

"Well, I don't want this anymore, Jerome. I'm tired. I'm exhausted. If it means I'm gonna die alone, then so be it. I'd rather be alone than be with you any longer." I've never heard myself speak so coldly to him before. But I can see that my words hit him; he takes an unsteady step back.

"What? What the hell does that mean?"

I try to ignore the distressed look on his face because if I do I might just take it all back.

"You can't do this to me!--To *us*, Dee. Please don't fucking do this."

Unable to help myself, I look him in the eye one last time.

"I'm sorry Jerome. I really am. *But get the hell out of my house*!"

CHAPTER TWO

His breath feels warm against my skin. It feels soft, like a caress. He runs his hands through my soft coily hair and it sends shivers through me. My breathing becomes erratic and my eyes close. His lips set out to explore every inch of my skin, leaving a trail of wet kisses in their wake, which are like a drug to me.

"Mhmhmm..." A breathy moan escapes my lips as a shudder ripples through me, he presses soft kisses into my neck. I've never felt this way even with Jerome. It had always been fast and rough and not in a good way but this man, someone I don't know, he takes his time.

Pulling away from me, he stares down at me and I finally see his face. Long blonde, nearly-silver hair drapes over his high cheekbones as he looks at me with piercing green eyes so deep it feels like he can see into the depths of my soul. He's so beautiful.

"You're so beautiful."

He takes the words out of my mouth as he gazes down at me in a way no one has ever looked at me before. Before I can reply, he silences me with his mouth. I feel myself burn with a need so intense that I wrap my arms around his neck and pull him down towards me so his lips meet mine in a fiery kiss.

He draws a trail of kisses from my neck, to my jaw, along the curve of my ear, and then down to my collarbone. My core tingles in anticipation as he reaches my navel.

Without a warning, he spreads my legs placing his hands on my thighs; he holds them in place and lowers his head. A hot breath of air hits my pussy and I can feel myself dripping in anticipation. His tongue flicks out, sending bolts of lightning as it darts across my insides. Feeling him so close makes me squirm.

I expect him to just eat me out and get it over with like how Jerome deals with it but again he takes his sweet time, placing chaste kisses on the insides of my thighs.

The man that's on top of me now doesn't seem to have anywhere else he needs to be and has all the time in the world for me as his breathing becomes heavy and he kisses me everywhere but where I want him to.

"Please," I moan out before I can stop myself, bucking my hips and wrapping my feet around him in an effort to get his mouth on me where I need it most. He pulls back, leaving me hanging with nothing but air and a thin line of spit to fill the space between us. My body is humming in anticipation and I respond by begging him over and over again, unable to formulate a coherent string of words.

His hot breath hits my exposed pussy as he replies, "Please what?" his tone slightly teasing, his hands holding me firmly in place while he looks at me expectantly.

His smooth, deep voice sends shivers down my spine.

"Please, please." I moan. And the sound of his low chuckle drives me crazy, but before I could finish my sentence, he gives me one deep lick against my pussy. The fire in my core leaps into a full blaze and I can feel myself getting wetter by the second.

His tongue is hot as it glides over my flesh and swollen lips. It dips inside me to lap up my juices before he wraps his lips around my clit.

As he sucks, one of his hands finds its way to my entrance, he slides a finger into me slowly while his gifted mouth continues teasing me, turning me into a puddle beneath him. My hips move against his mouth but he keeps me in place as I squirm in his hold.

Each lick and each thrust of his fingers bring me closer to the edge. The wet sounds of his hungry licking and growls mixed with my breathy moans drive me closer and closer...

He inserts another digit inside me, stretching me and I can't help but think of how it would feel once he's inside me. I can feel myself stretching as he explores deeper inside, swirling his finger in a clockwise direction. I grip onto the sheets as I moan louder now, it feels so good I can't stop myself from gasping for air.

"Ahhh... please don't stop." I whine, which only makes his movements faster. I feel my orgasm bubbling up inside me as my hips buck against him in desperate need. His hands continue stroking my insides before he grazes his teeth against my throbbing clit and that's all I need.

I can't control myself anymore... The wave breaks like an ocean surf crashing down onto the shore...

All of my muscles tighten at once and then release. A feeling so powerful flows through every nerve ending in my body as a scream erupts from my throat.

"Yes!" I scream and even as my orgasm dies down, he continues to suck, taking in every drop of my juices. He keeps moving his fingers in and out in slow movements.

The edges of my mind are foggy now...

Lifting his head from in between my legs, he reaches over and runs his fingers through my hair, looking back at me with those piercing green eyes, and for a split second, they flash a hot, blood red, his pupils thinning into slits before they return to their emerald green state.

I should be scared. But I don't feel any fear except for the anticipation of what he's planning to do to me next. He keeps his gaze on mine as he brings his fingers towards my mouth.

"Suck." He commands and normally I wouldn't follow a stranger's orders but the desire to please him overtakes me and so I part my lips, allowing him to place his glistening fingers on my tongue.

We don't break eye contact as I lick all of my wetness from his glistening fingers. He lets out a deep breath as I release them from my mouth with a pop.

"I want you inside me."

The orgasm he just gave me isn't enough.

I want more.

I can't help but want more.

He smirks at me, "Do you now?"

I nod, breathless.

"Your wish is my command."

Moving so smoothly that it almost seems inhuman, he nestles himself in between my legs, staring down at me with a look of lust and need. The air sizzles like someone took a hot iron to it, as his cock pushes up against my opening from underneath. I wait for him to ease himself into me but instead he slams against me.

"Ah!" I gasp sharply at the sudden but welcomed intrusion. He fills me up, stretching me to the point that it's almost painful.

He pauses for a second, watching my reaction as he pulls out before pushing himself back in, causing my toes to curl again at the feeling that's building up in my belly once more. As he thrusts into me, my walls grip onto him, almost afraid to let him go. I can feel myself stretch around him. His body is tight against mine and his muscles move like a well-oiled machine.

"Who do you belong to?"He asks, keeping himself steady yet deep inside me. I move my hips but he halts my movement, wrapping his fingers around my throat.

"I said, who do you belong to?" He repeats, his voice almost like a growl as his hold tightens at the base of my throat but doesn't suffocate me. His hold is solid and strong, but not painful. He rocks his hips and I'm forced to move with him or fall away.

In a haze of want, I answer: "I'm yours." My voice claws out of my throat, my words barely audible but I hope he understands.

He smiles and it takes my breath away.

I've never seen someone smile so beautifully before that I can't help but repeat;

"I'm all yours."

***

"I'm all yours," I say in a listless murmur as I slowly come awake, but when I open my eyes again, he's gone. I jolt up in bed.

The sun's just starting to rise, and the first bit of golden light peeks through the blinds.

There's a moment of disorientation as I try to figure out what just happened. Looking beside me, I expect the impossibly sexy stranger with green eyes to be there, but my bed is empty.

Throwing the quilted coverlet off of myself, I can see the evidence of what happened. There's a damp spot in the sheets below, and I can feel myself blushing as I realize that I must have had one of the most intense wet dreams of my life.

I touch my fingers to the fullness of my lips, still feeling the phantom sensation of his mouth on mine. They feel kiss-swollen. I close my eyes and try to will the handsome man back to me but he's gone.

It was just a dream.

A beautiful, amazing dream, but a dream nonetheless.

It's so strange since my dreams are rarely so vivid; in fact, normally I hardly ever remember them at all.

And then, everything that just happened the night before comes rushing back.

Jerome is gone. I found the courage to break free from him. Freedom has never felt so good before but, I still can't shake the feeling of his loss.

"Maybe that's why I dreamt up someone to keep me company. I'm not used to being alone..." I sink back down in my bed. It had felt all too real. Even now, I can still feel the cum soaking my panties.

I've always been restless, and sleeping beside Jerome certainly didn't help things, but today I feel refreshed.

I also still feel stretched, like my dream lover's dick was actually inside me. I can still feel his touch on my skin, his soft lips. My body is sticky with sweat and my arousal and my hair's a tangled mess. It was so real that I can't help but wonder if he was really here or not. Maybe this is just a sign that I need to get laid because, to be frank, Jerome wasn't good at a lot of things, and that included sex.

Getting out of bed, I let out a deep sigh. If only men like that actually existed, like the one in my dreams. How could someone be so beautiful and gentle yet rough in all the right ways?

Walking toward my window, I open the blinds so I can look out into the world, and I am greeted by the stillness of dawn. The sky is streaked with pink, blue, and orange, and the sun dominates half of the horizon with its cheerful warmth. My mind is still playing vivid flashbacks from last night when I realize:

"I didn't even get to cum with his dick!"

CHAPTER THREE

THE COFFEE SHOP ISN'T BIG, BUT IT'S IN A PRIME LOCATION. Its interior is painted light brown and the tables are made of dark mahogany wood. There's a counter to my left where a few baristas are rushing around, trying to make as many drinks as possible.

A lot of natural light seeps in through the windows, and it's enough to brighten the place up. The lights above glow and beneath their hanging lampshades. Painted elephants and wild roses grace the décor in shades of pink, gray, and blue.

The smoky aroma of roasted coffee beans, and the bittersweet scent of freshly baked muffins and pastries flakes through the air. I have to admit it is nice to be out and about after a few days of moping.

"You know the best thing about a break-up?" Beverly muses, she takes a sip from her skinny vanilla latte. She's sitting across from me on a stool, a small round table dividing us. I've never really cared about going to coffee shops, besides, I can always make my coffee at home but Bev despite being my best friend has always had a different outlook than me. And Beverly had insisted, so I finally gave in.

She loves going out into the hustle and bustle of people--and dragging me along with her. She is always on the go, anticipating the next new thing, whereas I am much more cautious. But sometimes I needed her to drag me out of hermit mode.

So I'd put on my favorite sundress, loving how the bright yellow accentuated my cinnamon brown skin, and some strappy flat sandals. Then I styled my tightly coiled hair in a half-up half-down do. With a top-knot above, and my cloud-like afro below. After applying my favorite cherry lip gloss, I'd slung a skinny strapped purse over my shoulder and went out before I could change my mind.

"What?" I ask.

"The rebound!" Her blue eyes flash mischievously, and the excited look on her face makes me roll my eyes. Of course she would say that. Beverly has always been a bit boy-crazy, and she's been anticipating my break up with Jerome since day one.

That's why we're even here. The minute I told her I had broken up with Jerome, she had demanded to see me right away for some 'sisterly advice.'

"I'm really not looking for a new relationship right now."

"Who said anything about a relationship? Girl, it's the 21st century." She tosses her sleek brown hair over a sun-tanned shoulder. "I don't think relationships are even a thing anymore. You just keep fucking until you find someone you want to fuck for a long time."

Then she shrugs. "You should really get with the program and stop playing around with *broke-ass dusties*."

I inhale deeply, and then exhale. Her words sting, but in a way they are true.

"You're right," I say to her, and shake my head; I never thought I would say this but she is.

I spent so much time investing in my relationships that I usually ended up getting the shorter end of the stick. It would be nice to find someone who actually gave a damn about me and had the means to do so. Or even a man I wouldn't have to save all the time.

But then again is it really worth the risk to try? Before I had met Jerome, all the other relationships I had been in were unfulfilling or just plain boring. *And even if I do meet someone interesting, who's to say they would even look my way?*

"I don't know..." I say. "Hook-ups? They're not really my thing."

Bev frowns at my response. "Don't give me that. This is what you always do."

"What are you talking about?"

"This!" She slams her palms on the table for emphasis. Drawing the attention of some of the other coffee shop patrons. "Ugh! I'm talking about you're whole: *'It's not really my thing,'* thing. I know you've always been cautious but come on, Deonne. You were the goddamn valedictorian, and you graduated the top of your class in an Ivy League school. More then that, you're drop-dead gorgeous! You're a fucking catch by any standard! Remember, you're the prize! So what the hell are you so scared of?"

She was right. It's just dating again, what the hell am I so scared of?

"Jerome! You can't keep doing this!" I shout as I stalk after his retreating figure. He doesn't stop. If anything, he quickens his pace. He thinks I'll give up, fall back and let him get away with his shitty behavior again.

"Jerome!" I shout, chasing after him and with purpose. "Jerome!"

He stops abruptly before turning back to me. His expression full of anger, his eyebrows furrowed, his jaw tight. His face is dark with stubble. "Keep doing what, Dee? Come on. Say what the fuck you want to my face!"

"You can't keep screwing up like this! This meeting was so important to me. I already told you that but instead of going

to your classes like you should be. You went out and got high with your friends."

"What? I'm not allowed to have fun? Is that what you want? For me to just stay home, go to school, find a job, and have nothing else in between?"

"I never said tha-"

"Because I'm not like you, Deonne. I'm not just some fucking loser who stays inside all the time."

"I never said that you couldn't go out! But you can't smoke your shit and get caught and expect ME to bail you out every time. This is the second time this year! You said you wouldn't let it happen again!"

"I'm fucking sorry then. Shit happens!" He exclaims with a shrug of his shoulders. And this would usually mean that he's done with the conversation but I just am not.

"Yeah, shit happens. Like the shit at work that I have to fix because I have to take care of you."

Jerome scoffs as he gives me an unimpressed look. "Are you serious? Take care of me? What? Do you think you're doing me a favor? Who the hell do you think you are?"

He stalks towards me with an amused expression and suddenly all the words in my mouth die out.

"You're nothing without me, Deonne. Do you think someone else would put up with all your bullshit? You can have your degrees, apartment or your nice job but that doesn't take away what you really are, just a sad little girl who no one else will love."

"Deonne!" I'm snapped out of my thoughts as Bev snaps her brightly polished fingers in my face.

"I'm serious! What are you so afraid of? You're beautiful, sweet, and not to mention the smartest girl I know. You're a bad bitch, any man would be lucky to even spend a night with you!"

I chuckle softly. As much as I would like to believe her, I just can't.

For Bev, love is an adventure to be conquered. Fighting dragons and overcoming insurmountable odds is just a typical day in her world. She has always wanted me to be more like her. Bev's partner in crime, but I could never quite reach her level of confidence.

"Come on girl, at least give it a chance. You can't spend too much time wasting away just because of that freeloading asshole. Are you really going to let him affect you any more than he already has? You gonna just lay down and let him win?"

A flash of fury courses through me. He has already taken enough, I can't keep living like this. And if I don't start now, I'll just end up repeating the same cycle.

"No!" I say, indignant.

"That's the spirit! Fuck him and fuck his stupid broke-ass friends. Find someone actually worthy of you." She cheers as she takes another sip from her latte. "And I know the perfect way you can start. We're going to get you out and about again." A cheeky smirk forms on her face and for a second I hesitate.

"Oh god...how?" I ask despite myself. I have learned over time that sometimes it is better to just go along with her crazy schemes.

She beams at me as she raises her arm up in the air to get the attention of the barista.

"What's this about?" I ask as Beverly turns from me and waves the lanky barista over to the table.

"Can I get another round of lattes over here? Make it a double this time, my girl's gonna need it."

"You have got to be fucking kidding me," I say with a sigh, feeling myself sink in my seat.

He nods with a smile, and a wink before he heads to the espresso maker behind him. Beverly's eyes are dancing now as she looks over at me. "So what do you think?"

"The barista?" I ask frowning. "Look, Bev. He's...not my type, like, at all."

"No, not him! What I mean is there's this single's mixer that's happening tonight. A lot of rich guys and hot dudes are apparently going to be there." She explains, and for some reason I have a feeling that she had already planned this long before the breakup. "And I've already signed you up."

Of course she did.

CHAPTER FOUR

"What do single people usually wear?"

I muse to myself, staring at my powder blue bra and panties-clad body in the full-length mirror.

And, I was still debating on whether or not I should wear my hair down or up, extensions or no. Jerome always preferred the extensions. I realize I'm not really sure what I even liked anymore. I'm so confused.

Jerome had a lot of demands about how I should dress, I suddenly realize. I had forgotten the styles I actually like on me.

After hanging out with Beverly, I went home to get ready for the mixer. I've never gone out to anything like this before so I figured I would need the extra time to choose what to wear.

And I was definitely right.

Nosing through my closet, I'm greeted by all the office attire that I usually wear. I'm not really the party or the going out type so I haven't really had the need for anything too flashy, not since my clubbing days anyways. And even though I tried to keep on top of my workout schedule, being in a relationship with Jerome made me settle into a more sedentary routine, they'd be a bit tight now. Relationship weight really is a thing.

"I have to have at least a dress somewhere in here," I mumble to myself as I ruffle through the countless blouses, knee-length pencil skirts and square pants that I commonly use in the office when I finally found it.

"This is perfect!" I pull out a flattering short flowy smoky plum-colored dress. It was a gift from Beverly. She had said that the color matched my mocha skin and I agreed with her completely but I had never gotten the chance to wear it until now. Jerome had said it made me look trashy and dresses like this didn't suit me and stupid me believed it.

Shrugging on the dress, it falls to my thighs, hugging my curves comfortably as the neckline dips revealing a sultry hint of cleavage. Admiring myself in the mirror, I nod my head in approval.

This is perfect.

I put on a thin drop chain necklace to complement the outfit before shrugging on a pair of simple black pumps.

I leave my curly hair as it is, letting it fall in coily springs against my shoulders before swiping a thin layer of tinted lip gloss over my pouty lips. Taking one more look in the mirror, I smile to myself.

This is going to be my night.

The mixer is at a Four Seasons Hotel, I've been to the Hotel chain only a few times before--and only ever on business. The hotel sprawls up and down the block, leading me to believe that it is on the tallest building in the city.

As I make my way through the front doors, I am immediately hit with the smell of fresh-cut roses, cinnamon and peppermint. Everything looks luxurious and expensive. The entrance to the hotel is all glass, the fountain's lights reflecting in the glass high-ceilings, allowing me a glimpse of the universe above.

The walls of the lobby are made of ebony with gold borders and the flooring is mahogany lined with plush white carpet runners.

Beverly had texted me the address and when I arrived at the lobby, butterflies erupt in my stomach. I can't believe I'm really doing this. Especially since it's just been just a short while since my breakup with Jerome.

A moment of hesitation hits me but I quickly shrug it off. There's no use turning back now because if I do it would mean that Jerome wins and I wasn't letting that happen, not over my dead body.

Lifting my chin up, I let out a shaky breath as I step towards the receptionist.

"I'm here for the mixer?"

The receptionist looks up with a smile as she points towards a long hallway. "Last door in the right is the event's room. You won't miss it."

"Thank you." I nod my head gratefully as I walk towards the direction she pointed to.

"Good luck! Hope you find what you're looking for!" She calls out.

I hope so too.

Entering the room, the chatter of people greets my ears, interspersed with the clink of glasses. My heart pounds against my chest, drumming against my ears as I look around at the wave of single men and women. A lot of them were already mingling. Some had taken to eating with a partner that they already found while the others indulge in simple conversation as they enjoyed their drinks from the open bar.

A small fleet of waiters is scurrying back and forth across the room, bearing trays laden with newly-filled plates. The lights are dimmed to set the tone.

A small orchestra plays on the left side of the room: a pianist tinkling out soft melody on their ivories, a violinist sawing out a tune, a drummer keeping their rhythm, while the saxophonist's mellifluous and smooth melody flows like water over pebbles, completing a gorgeous soft jazzy tune.

The realization comes to me in a sudden epiphany: I'm in over my head.

Gaze darting around the room, I quickly try to find a place where I won't stick out. Which would defeat the purpose of coming here but my nerves just can't handle it especially since I didn't see even one familiar face.

Speed walking to the buffet, I keep myself busy by trying to look for a plate. They should really keep them somewhere more accessible, but I'm just thankful that I have something to do instead of just standing around looking crazy as I wait for someone to approach me.

Unable to find any, I sigh in defeat, deciding to just order something from the bar, I turn around only to bump into a hard wall. I stumble back, but instead of bumping into the table behind me, a pair of strong hands hold me steady by my shoulders.

"Are you okay?"

That voice sounds so familiar. Looking up, my breath hitches as my eyes widen with recognition at the same pair of captivating green eyes from my dreams. I realize it's him, only, his powerful body isn't fully on display, this time, he's dressed in a designer suit, yet still managing to keep an understated look.

But, that's impossible!

I am definitely not okay. I'm hallucinating. I have to be. This is just my imagination playing games with me.

Come on, Deonne. Stop blinking at him and say something!

"Um...yes, I-I am." But I feel like I'm gonna faint, and the words come stiffly with my shock.

Deep green eyes scan over me, taking in my appearance. I can feel them move their way over the outline of my body.

"Are you *sure* you're okay?" The deep huskiness of his voice makes my knees weak. I nod my head, trying to find the courage to speak.

"Yes, yes. I'm fine, thank you. You kinda saved me before I could make a complete fool of myself." I say.

He lets out a rich chuckle as he smiles down at me, making my heart flutter.

This can't be happening.

"I wouldn't usually care this much, but it's my fault you're in my arms. I wasn't looking where I was going. I'm sorry." But his eyes are nothing but unapologetic as they travel over me without reserve. A rush of heat goes through me, settling in my lower belly. By now, I am near enough so that only a few inches separate us. I swallow hard as I meet his eyes again and lick my lips unconsciously, and he follows the movement, his eyes growing dark. Instantly I feel butterflies taking flight in my stomach.

"I'm Rafael by the way. Had I met you under better circumstances, I would have said something a lot smoother, but..." He says, his voice velvety smooth, then he shrugs with a slow smile. "I'll take what I can get."

His smile is breathtaking; the curve of his lips forms a perfect line, accentuating his jaw and highlighting the bow of his full lips. It's warm and inviting, and the more I stared at it, the more I wanted to have those lips on mine.

He smells like heaven. His cologne is light and musky, mixing with his own scent.

I want to lean in close and take a big whiff, but I'm afraid I'll lose my ability to stand. I can't move. I'm trapped by the intensity of his gaze, and there's nothing I can do but stare right back.

Rafael tilts his head, raising a brow as he waits for me to say something as nervousness overcomes me. My heart is hammering against my chest, my palms are getting sweaty, and I can't think of anything to say.

"I'm Deonne," I answer back finally, and then realize I have no idea what to say next.

But I don't have to say anything else. He leans closer, and for a second I think he's going to kiss me, but he just moves one of his hands from my shoulder to my elbow, giving it a gentle squeeze; it's as if his warmth flows into me.

"I'm glad to meet you, Deonne," he says, his voice soft and velvety. I'm in a trance as I deep into his eyes. My heart skips a beat, and I can feel my cheeks flush with heat.

"Would you let me buy you a drink to make up for it?"

Still in shock that what I thought was nothing but a fantasy is actually real, I swallow thickly and nod my head.

Girl, get a grip. I chide myself, and I manage a sultry smirk back at him. "Well. I can't really say no to a free drink, can I?"

CHAPTER FIVE

"So you're telling me that a guy like you has never had a girlfriend before?"

"Okay, okay," Rafael laughs lightly, as he takes a sip of his whisky on the rocks. "I can see how you'd think that, but seriously, I've never had a girlfriend before."

He must see my look of sheer skepticism because he adds:

"Come on, Deonne. Would I lie?"

"Well, this is the first time I've met you, so I call bullshit." The corner of my mouth turns up slightly as the lemon drop martini I'm nursing lands back on the counter with a tink.

It can't be true, and if it is, well that's a big fat red flag! I think to myself and wait for his explanation.

"Your lack of trust stings, Deonne." He says, placing a hand against his heart, feigning hurt. "But yes, I stand by it. Sure, I've had a couple of hook-ups but my work usually keeps me so busy that I've never had time to actually talk to the women I meet, much less go on a date."

"Well, that I can relate to. What do you do?"

"I just manage a small company. It's not really important, and I don't want to talk about work right now." He brushes the topic off and although a part of me wants to dig deeper, I let it slide. I can understand wanting to escape from your job from time to time.

"Besides, what I'm more interested in is how a girl like you is still single."

"A girl like me?" I question, wondering what he means.

"Drop-dead fucking gorgeous."

His words have me choking on my cocktail as I set it down. "Well, aren't you forward?"

The smile he gives me is just decadent; rough, manly, and sensual. I feel a jolt in my chest. There's a storm within his deep green eyes, and he looks at me with undisguised hunger.

"Not really, just honest. So what's the story behind that?" He asks, leaning against the counter as he studies me and I almost want to cover myself from his hooded gaze. I'm not quite sure if it's the intense green of his eyes, but it feels like he's staring deep into me, like he can see past the surface.

"Just the usual. Bad taste in men. He's not important anymore, and I don't really want to talk about it." I repeat his words and he shrugs in response.

"Fair enough. I don't really want to talk about other guys anyway, but for what it's worth he's completely dense for letting you go."

"You really think so?"

"I know so." He reassures, and his smile seems to wash away all the insecurities that Jerome has instilled in me over the years. I should have met him way sooner.

Standing up, Rafael offers me his hand. "Come on," He nods his head at the mostly empty dance floor. "Let's dance."

Placing my hand in his, hesitantly, I feel him enclose his own around it and I'm met with the feeling of rightness from before.

"Sure." I find myself smiling.

Upbeat jazz fills the room with a hypnotic beat and I let the melody take me, I sway and sashay my hips in time with the rhythm, with a light laugh. A few guys, come over to dance with me and although I try to entertain them, Rafael seems to drive them off with his presence alone. His eyes almost glow, the deep green of an emerald. They could hypnotize me if I let them.

As if staking his claim, he places a hand on my waist, drawing me closer to his chest as our hips sway to the beat. The crowd fades away as he moves me so that I'm facing him. Smoothly as a man can be, he pulls me in closer and starts to dance along with me, and we move as one. Our bodies sway together as if we've done this before.

"I didn't know you could dance." I lean forward so he can hear me and he lowers himself so I can reach him.

"There's a lot of things you don't know about me yet, Deonne. And there are a lot of things I can do." His hand drops from my waist to cup my ass as he squeezes it gently. He winks back and my stomach flutters at his words. "I can show you sometime if you'd like."

Our bodies flow together, making a rhythm all on their own with their own melody and harmony, the notes that come from the two of us in motion together. His hand goes from my waist up to my neck, and I feel myself get flush from head to toe under his touch—that's when he makes his move—when we're already so close and still wrapped up in the moment—he leans down and brushes his lips against mine. And it's electric.

The next thing I know, I'm pressed up against one of the hotel room doors, his lips against my neck as he fumbles for his key card.

"Mhmmm...Rafael." I breathe out as he sucks on the sweet spot where my shoulder meets my neck. I don't even hear the card activate as the door swings open. Pushing me inside, he closes the door behind him and looks at me like he wants to absolutely ravish me.

The room is dark but the windows are open, allowing a bit of moonlight to stream in, just enough for me to see his handsome features and his mesmerizing eyes.

"Tonight, I'll make you forget any man who came before me. I'll show you what real pleasure feels like."

For a second, his deep green eyes flash red again like from my dreams but in my lust-filled haze, I can't bring myself to care. That was for the morning. Tonight, I just want to see all the things he can do to me.

Closing the space between us, he whips off my dress over my head, tossing it to the side, leaving me in my underwear. I'm so glad that I wore a matching pair.

"Fuck, you're beautiful." He breathes out huskily as he nudges my chin upward, bringing his mouth to mine in a soft kiss. His mouth covers mine and we move together in sync. I yield to his kiss and arch my back, yearning for more skin-to-skin contact and he pins me down into the bed's springy mattress. Underneath his shirt, he feels hard, muscular, and warm. He breaks away from me and stands above me with his legs between mine, as if ready to pounce on his prey.

In a surprising wave of confidence, I unhook my bra, letting my breasts spill out, my dark nipples erect in the cold and the anticipation. "So what are you waiting for? Show me what you can do."

He smirks and the light-hearted Rafael from earlier dissipates because now he seems more like a beast than a man, "Well then...don't mind if I do."

Running his hands against my thighs, expert fingers find the hem of my panties, tugging them down over my legs slowly, letting them drop to the floor, leaving me completely naked before him.

Spreading my legs, he stares down at my pussy, his eyes almost glowing in the dim lighting. The smirk on his lips never leaving his face. "Beautiful, and wet." He grunts as he places a finger against my aching core.

I move my hips for more friction but he holds me down in place. "Stop. Don't make me tie you up." He demands and my movements cease instantly in submission.

"You're not allowed to move until I tell you to. Is that clear?"

"Yes."

"Good girl." He runs his hands over my wet pussy, taking his time as he lets his fingers trace every inch of me while I try not to squirm against his hold. I've been waiting for this night ever since I had that dream and every minute he spends teasing me just makes me even wetter.

"Please..." I whimper.

"Please what?" He pinches my clit and a soft squeal escapes me.

"Please fuck me already!" I gasp out, and he doesn't need to be told twice. Withdrawing his hand, he unbuckles his belt, letting his pants fall to the ground to reveal his member, large, thick, heavy, and already erect and I can't help but lick my lips.

He removes his shirt, tossing it to the side to reveal his hard abs. I had a feeling he would be fit when I bumped into him, but I never expected him to look almost perfect. I spread my legs in invitation.

Grabbing both my wrists with one hand he pins them over my head as he places himself in between my thighs. The tip of his hard cock throbs against my entrance, I feel heat radiating from him like hot iron, but he doesn't sink himself into me yet. I rock my hips, desperate to feel him inside me, but he lets out an animalistic growl.

"What did I say?"

My movements cease immediately as he continues to tease me with the tip of his member. Another whimper escapes me when suddenly he rams himself inside me, filling me up like in my dreams.

"Rafael!" I gasp at the sudden intrusion but he doesn't allow me to adjust. He begins thrusting in me.

He wastes no time, and pounds into me mercilessly. He thrusts deeply, angling his hips for the deepest penetration. Helpless, my fingers tremble as I throw my head back from the force of his thrusts. His mouth covers mine as he continues his assault on my pussy, until a muffled cry leaves me.

"Ahhh..." All I could do is mewl and moan in pleasure as he continues to use me. The fires of passion burn within and I struggle to find air under his weight as I spasm and quiver, my body absolutely electrified by his touch. Sliding his hand down to rub at my clit, he pinpoints the bundle of nerves with ruthless precision until I feel a scream building up in my throat, the orgasm bursts out of me in a sudden release of pleasure and pain, and I scream out.

"Fuck!-" he thunders and lifts my leg to plant it on his shoulder for a deeper angle. With a feral groan, he shoves his thick, hard cock deeper inside of me. "I love it when you scream," he tells me hoarsely.

My hands grip the sheets as moan after moan escapes me. Leaning down, he places his lips on mine never ceasing his movements as our lips move in unison.

The taste of his mouth, the dizzying scent of his skin, and the feel of his hands on me all become one. He trails kisses from my lips to my throat and back again, making me squirm under his weight. He finally lets go of my hands, allowing me to wrap them around his neck as he cups my breast into his palm, tweaking my nipple. And still, he slams into me without mercy, showing no restraint as he fucks me like an absolute animal.

Another orgasm builds on the heels of the last, my heart is racing in my chest and I know that I can't hold on much longer.

"Come for me, baby." He commands. His voice is thick with lust, the desire in his eyes ignites even more flames of desire within me. It pushes me over the edge. The pleasure is so intense, it has become almost unbearable, but the pain takes me over the edge and I come crashing down from the high that I am soaring on.

"Rafael!" I moan out as a wave of pleasure courses through me, gushing around him. Rafael doesn't stop his thrusts. Working his hips faster, he fills me with a second rush of climactic ecstasy. I moan louder and it only spurs him on.

"Fuck, baby. I'm gonna cum." Rafael throws himself into me with a final thrust, shoving all of his long thick dick deep inside as he explodes inside of me. The feeling of his hot seed pouring into me almost sets off another orgasm but I can't quite reach it. Normally, I would get mad considering he doesn't have a condom, but I can't seem to find it in my head to care just now.

I watch him reach his climax, almost mesmerized as his eyes flash red. What could that even possibly be? I can't think of any logical reason but logic escapes me right now.

Placing another soft kiss on my lips, Rafael pulls out of me. Rolling to the side so he can lay beside me, he strokes my cheek and smiles seductively. Now I know that it wasn't my mind playing games with me, his eyes actually glow red for a moment.

What the actual fuck? Why do they do that?

We both pant heavily, soaking up the after-glow of sex.

"Were you impressed?" He asks huskily with a smile while he caresses my exposed skin, leaving a trail of fire behind. I squirm under his touch, and giggle, my face flushed.

Almost breathless with desire, I murmur back to him. "You were alright. But I didn't really get to judge you that well. Maybe I need another demonstration?"

Rafael chuckles as he grabs my thigh and pulls me towards him. "Whatever the lady wishes. Just make sure to pay attention this time."

CHAPTER SIX

M OST DAYS WHEN I WAS STILL WITH JEROME, I WOULD WAKE UP TO THE SOUND OF HIM STILL PLAYING GAMES ON THE FLAT SCREEN WITH HIS FRIENDS. I'd have to make him something to eat before I could get ready for work. But today is a different day. This morning, I'm woken up by soft rays of sunlight peeking through the curtains and the scent of breakfast wafting around the room.

Opening my eyes, I expect to be back in my bedroom but instead, I'm greeted by the hotel room and shirtless, Rafael standing over me with two cups of coffee in hand. He takes a sip from one while the other he offers me.

"Morning, beautiful." He greets me as I sit up, accepting the drink. Reaching out, I realize he'd put me in a silk kimono robe. I must've had the deepest most restful sleep of my life. I take a sip of hot, strong coffee and sigh in contentment as the tension leaves my body. But as scenes of last night's event flash through my mind, a deep blush coats my cheeks.

"Good morning," I reply my voice hoarse, probably from all the screaming I'd done earlier. He takes a seat beside me, placing a hand on my thigh, and I lean back into Rafael's strong chest as we drink in comfortable silence.

I could really get used to this.

"You hungry? I got room service. I wasn't sure what you would want so I just ordered everything on the breakfast menu." He gestures to a trolley on the side of the bed, filled with different types of food.

My eyes widen in surprise. "Are you serious? That's gotta be expensive." I can't help but comment as he chuckles.

"Don't worry about it." He says dismissively bringing the trolley over. Grabbing a plate of omelets, he cuts into it with a fork, before balancing it delicately before me like an offering to a goddess.

"Say 'ahh'," He smiles and I open my mouth for him to feed me. He feeds me like a child, making sure that nothing spills on me.

"That's delicious." I gasp as the flavor hits my tongue.

"I know, that's why I chose this hotel." He says before taking a bite for himself.

Chose this hotel? Wasn't it just a coincidence since the mixer had been held here?

"Rafael, what do you mean you *chose* this hotel?" I ask but before he can answer, the door's buzzer rings.

"Hold that thought." Passing me the plate so I can continue eating, Rafael gets up and pulls the door open, and a woman in a black-and-white uniform stands with a few bags in hand.

"Hello, Sir. Here are the clothes that you've requested."

Clothes? Why would he request clothes?

My eyes narrow as I chew slower, studying the situation before me when my phone starts going off. My purse is hanging off the headboard, and I fish the vibrating phone out. A notification with Jerome's name flashes across the screen and dread settles in my stomach. I hesitate for a moment before unlocking the screen.

Immediately, my eyes widen in horror as I see the countless messages he's sent me since last night. All of them are angry and full of profanities, demanding to know where I am. One message said that I was nothing but a tool to get him ahead in his career and that he never loved me. He's called me every name in the book, telling me that I'm a slut and a whore...and the last few, they border on threatening, and violent.

My hands start shaking as the tears fill my eyes and I drop the phone on the bed.

"Is there anything else I can assist you with?" The worker's voice drifts to me from the hotel's room door.

"No, I'll call you if we need anything else. Thanks." Rafael grabs the bags from her, and hands her a tip before closing the door with a hollow thud.

In her place, he stands with a triumphant and impish smirk on his face. But as soon as he sees my expression, his features soften in concern. I avert my gaze, I can feel Rafael's eyes on me but I can't bring myself to look at him. I'm embarrassed, humiliated, and heartbroken all at the same time.

Without a word, Rafael drops the bags and takes the plate of food away from me before gently putting his arms around me. I can't hold back anymore and I sob into his chest as he strokes my hair, letting everything out. He doesn't say anything, he just lets me cry it out until I have nothing left.

Eventually, I pull away from him and wipe my face with the silky sleeve of my robe. "I'm sorry." I sniffle, trying to compose myself.

"For what?" He asks, tenderly cupping my face in his hands.

"For everything! For ruining our breakfast. And for being such a damn mess—" I reply, fresh tears threatening to fall.

He smiles and kisses me lightly on the forehead. "Don't be sorry. Not for one second."

Jerome's face flashes through my mind and I shudder. "I don't want to see him or talk to him ever again," I say honestly, glaring bitterly at the phone beside me.

"It's alright. I'll take care of that. I'll take care of everything."

That was impossible of course, but Rafael's voice, and the low rumble in his chest is so soothing, in that moment, I'd take it as a substitute. Slipping from his hold, I push myself upright, sobering enough to notice the designer shopping bags that Rafael has brought into the room with him.

"What'd you do?" I ask slowly. I'm not sure if I should be pissed or touched. Rafael's smile returns.

"You can take a shower. I got you a change of clothes. You probably don't want to wear your dress from last night and I don't think you'd want to wear my clothes where I'm planning to take you."

"Planning to take me? We're going somewhere?"

Plus I thought I'd definitely scared him off with my tearful breakdown.

"Well... I thought since we skipped the date part,--And believe me, I never planned on that-- We could make up for it. I have the whole day planned out." He leaves my side to pick up the paper bags by their woven handles and places them on the bed. "And, I figured you could take your mind off things."

I should be mad that he's planning everything without even consulting me but it's nice to have someone think for me for a change. Instead of me just needing to take care of someone. It's too bad that in a couple of hours, I have to leave.

"I'm not sure if I can go. I have work today." I reply, and my voice cracks. Rubbing the last of the tears from my eyes, I smile my feigned enthusiasm at him. The carpet feels so soft under my feet, I'm tempted to just curl up and stay here forever. I can't believe that it's been such a rollercoaster of a morning.

I feel Rafael's hard gaze on me for a long moment. "Call them. Ask for the day off. In fact, ask for the week off."

I laugh in his face at his words, expecting him to be joking but he only looks at me with a serious expression.

He isn't joking.

"Are you insane? I don't know where you work, Rafael, but that is not the kind of thing I can pull at my job."

I truly wish I could spend more time with this man. Hell, I wish I could wake up in his arms every morning but he's a fling, a stranger. And even if I haven't had a vacation since graduating college, what if my workplace doesn't let me? They've come to expect me to be around, in fact, with all the co-workers I help, you'd think I'd have a higher position by now. There's even a promotion I've been gunning for all year. Asking for time off would definitely halt that train right in its tracks.

Sure, the thought of going on a date with Rafael was exhilarating but I can't get away with it. I've never heard of anyone taking so much time off from work.

Sensing my apprehension, he goes on.

"Just trust me. Would it hurt to try?" He looks at me with those mesmeric eyes. I'm lost in them before I realize he's asking me a question.

I suppose he has a point, I suppose it won't hurt to ask for a single day. I definitely wouldn't ask for a week though. Now that'd be crazy.

"Fine. I don't think it'll work, but I'll try." I concede, but he seems pleased. Reaching for my phone, I dial for my boss's office. It rings a few times before he picks up.

"Deonne! How are we with that presentation for next week?"

"Everything is all set, sir. I have all of it in the flash drive on my computer...but I--" I venture tentatively, and feel my voice waver, my hand twitching nervously on my thigh. I can't bring myself to admit that I am actually calling about something else. My voice is caught in my throat.

I freeze, turning to Rafael, suddenly unsure. He waves a hand telling me to go on. I can't believe I'm doing this. I can't even remember the last time I requested a day off. And my boss, although tolerable, isn't the most understanding.

"--That's great. You know what, take the day off."

My eyes widen. "S-sir?" I stammer.

"Take the day off, Deonne. You deserve it. In fact, take the whole week off."

"A-are you joking?"

"I'm not. You've worked your butt off for the last few years and it occurred to me, I don't think I've ever seen you take a single vacation. You're already a sure candidate for that promotion you've been working towards and we can surely manage without you for a week. So go have fun."

Without even letting me get a word in, he hangs up the phone. I gape at Rafael who only smiles at me innocently.

"So?" He asks, the smile never leaving his face. "What'd your workplace say?"

I can't believe it. I'm free for an entire week.

"I have the day off...I have the whole week off, actually." I say, unable to believe my own words. I'm still gaping when he places a hand on my chin and closes my mouth.

"You did it. You're free. We can go on the trip I planned then. Hurry up and eat. I'll finalize all the arrangements while you finish up."

This is going on so well. A little bit too well.

Standing up, he places a swift kiss on my lips but before he can leave, I grab him by his arm.

"Do you have something to do with this?" I ask clutching onto him.

"Me? How can I? I don't even know where you work." His tone is innocent but my mind can't help but run in circles. I can't stop thinking about the fact that the first time I met him was in my dreams or the fact that his eyes seem to change color.

And he's just perfect. Too perfect.

"You have a point." I let go of him, and he straightens himself up, flashing me a grin.

"Just think of it as...magic."

CHAPTER SEVEN

"**W**HERE ARE YOU EVEN TAKING ME?" I ask, adjusting the pink ombre Rayban frames over my eyes as we step out into the sunlit lot of the hotel. He'd even got my favorite color right. Rafael opens the door to a BMW, allowing me to step inside before jogging to the driver's side.

"It's a surprise" He answers simply, not offering any more information.

My mother always warned me about stranger danger but maybe it's because I've already met him in my dreams that I feel no hint of fear or even doubt that he would ever do something to hurt me.

Although I can't help but be suspicious of him...or what he actually is. In fact, that's partially why I wore these sunglasses, to casually steal glances at him without him taking notice.

We drive at a steady drift. It's nice being in the passenger's seat for once, in the hands of a capable driver. He places a hand on my thigh while he keeps the other steady on the wheel. My mind races with thoughts about him, and every strange coincidence surrounding him but I'm promptly disrupted when I feel his hand starting to rise.

My breath hitches when he runs his hand beneath my skirt, and against the hem of my panties. I look in his direction, he keeps his eyes on the road but he doesn't stop moving his fingers. His fingers find their way to my clit, and my whole body tenses in massive anticipation.

"Shouldn't you be focusing on the road?" My voice is a breathless whisper.

"I am. I don't know what you're talking about," he says, his expression completely collected, he keeps his movements slow and steady. With his eyes on the road, his fingers never stop. I want to protest, but his fingers are teasing my clit so deliciously, causing my brain to go blank. I want to ask him a hundred questions. But I can't bring myself to do it. Not yet. Right now, I just want to enjoy this moment. I want to enjoy him.

I can feel my panties getting damper by the second, and the way he's playing with my clit. Slow circles trace the bundle of nerves, and I know it won't be long. I bite my bottom lip, trying to keep the moans in my throat, but he isn't playing that game.

"I can hear you, you know." He says huskily, speeding up his movements, and the car down the highway. "The more you try to stay quiet, the more it turns me on."

"Mhmm-" A soft moan escapes me while I grab onto the car seat's leather.

I bite down harder on my lip and his fingers just press a little harder, working my clit with just the right amount of pressure. I can feel the tide rising and I press my back against the seat, trying to keep my body from moving too much.

My eyes flutter close and I let the gentle pleasure wash over me. Rafael brings me to a soft orgasm and my body reaches complete relaxation in the afterglow of the climax. I don't even notice that he's already parked the car. Opening my eyes just in time to see him suck his finger clean, he turns toward me with a wink.

"Just in time."

Looking around, I see that we're at the airport. A second later, he helps me out of the car, and I wrap my arms around his neck like a scarf.

I kiss him, and nip on his bottom lip and I can feel him harden under me. It's not enough. It's not nearly enough.

His hands grab my bottom and I gasp into his mouth when I feel him grind into me. But before he can get too carried away, he breaks the kiss, and I nearly whimper.

"We gotta go." He says, giving me a peck on my lips before letting me slide down to my feet. He picks up the bags, and I follow him to the terminal building.

Inside, people are bustling to and from gates, a mass of humanity like a cloud of beige and gray suit jackets, who never quite climb the sky.

Rafael's eyes divert to my body and his hands reach out to grab my hips as he pulls me closer to him.

"Rafael? Where are we going?" I panic when it sinks in that we would be potentially leaving the state.

He smiles. "We're going to Hawaii!"

I never thought I would have the chance to go to Hawaii but here I am, in a bikini I could never afford to splurge on with the man of my dreams, literally, walking along the sands of gold on the beach. Rafael rented a catamaran and we ride out to the reef where the water is clear enough for us to see the colorful schools of fish underneath rippling waves.

White wine, chicken salad sandwiches, and fruits on ice cool us as we sun. I burst into guffaws basking in the warm sun, laughing so hard that tears stream down my face.

Back on the shore, we watch the sun start to set and the sound of the waves lulls me to a state of peace. Rafael holds my hand tightly in his as we walk by the sea.

Rafael ended up renting an entire beach house for us, where a good chunk of the land is considered private property so we can see no one for miles.

"You know most people bring girls to the movies for a first date. Not fucking Hawaii." I chuckle while Rafael smirks.

"Well, I'm not most people. I'm better than any man you'll ever meet, baby."

"Cocky much?"

"Not cocky, just honest," Rafael smirks.

"I disagree, you're very much...cock-y." I wink while Rafael laughs.

He rounds on me, his eyes darkening. "Say that word again." He demands, his voice husky and I have an idea what he means.

"What? Cock?" I repeat, and Rafael growls and lets out a deep breath.

"I like dirty words in your mouth. They sound so sexy." He groans.

"You know what else would be sexy in my mouth?" I ask.

"What?" He asks, holding my hips.

"Your cock." I say, slowly with a sultry tone. I feel my cheeks heat up as Rafael's gaze holds me mesmerized by his gaze.

"Don't tease me, baby." Rafael's voice is deep and I could feel the heaviness in his voice. The sound pulls me and I feel my body respond to him. I don't think I can help it. In his eyes, there is a fire that burns a bit brighter, a bit hotter than before.

Without another word, I lower myself to my knees, looking up at Rafael as he breathes heavily in anticipation.

He tangles his fingers into the springy softness of my hair as I pull down his swim shorts, allowing his already hard dick to spring free.

Keeping my eyes on him, I let my tongue trail from the base of his dick to the tip, tasting the slight salt of pre-cum. Rafael moans as I slowly run my tongue down the shaft. I wrap my lips around his dick.

"Mmm...fuck." He moans, gripping my hair tighter and I respond by slowly trying to get his full length into my mouth. He is so big.

He stares down at me with half-lidded eyes, while his free hand strokes my cheek lovingly.

Hollowing my cheeks, I suck as I let my tongue swirl around. His hips thrust into my mouth and I follow his pace, bobbing my head to his rhythm.

I can feel the tip of his dick hit the back of my throat and I concentrate on not choking. I've never been this deep before, but for him I will.

My jaw starts to ache but I have no choice but to hold him down. I don't want to stop. I want to know that I can make him feel this good.

"Fuck, Deonne. Don't stop." He groans as his thrusts become more erratic and I feel his cock twitch. I prepare myself for his load.

"I'm gonna come—" He murmurs, spilling his seed, and I feel his warm, sticky cum shoot down my throat and I swallow every drop of it, sucking as I do so. His hips jerking as he holds my head in place.

Letting his cock go with a pop of my mouth, I take a deep breath looking up at Rafael as he pants heavily from the intensity of his orgasm.

Smirking, I rise to my feet and plant a quick kiss on his lips. "Thanks for the meal."

CHAPTER EIGHT

"I HAD AN AMAZING TIME." I smile as Rafael walks me to the door of my apartment while I fumble for my keys.

"Can I ask for a next time?" He arches a brow at me when I look up at him. "I mean...I don't want to seem presumptuous... I know we just met."

He looks at me with an almost boyish smile that tugs at my heartstrings.

When I hear his words, I don't know how to feel. I mean, he's handsome and so charming, and the best lover I've ever had--there's no denying that. But I don't know if I'm ready for a relationship. My last one was not a good one, and I don't know if I can ever really get over it. I don't know if I can trust again. And I don't know if I can give myself over to someone who could potentially hurt me. I'm not sure if I can take another heartbreak.

I need to be honest with him and let him know how I feel. "I don't think I'm ready for a relationship. I'm...really sorry." I tell him, watching his brows furrow at my honesty.

He takes my hand and presses a kiss to my palm. "That's alright, Deonne. We're just taking it slow. No pressure."

He leans in and presses a kiss to my lips. "Call me when...if you're ready."

"I will," I whisper in response.

"Hopefully sooner than later." He winks at me before turning and walking away, leaving me standing there with my heart pounding in my chest.

Finding my keys, I gaze at them for a small eternity, then turn back to watch Rafael's retreating back, with a feeling of intense longing.

After this, everything would go back to normal. The man of my dreams might just walk around the corner and out of my life forever.

And before I even realize it, I take a step forward, then another and another, until I'm running after him, calling his name.

"Rafael! Wait!"

He turns back to look at me with a questioning expression, but I don't give him a chance to say anything. I crash into him, throwing my arms around his neck and kissing him with all the pent-up passion and desire that I feel.

He responds eagerly, wrapping his arms around me and picking me up so that my legs are wrapped around his waist.

"Just one last night?" I whisper against his lips.

"One last night." He agrees, his voice husky.

He kisses me deeply, both of us frantic with need for each other, as he carries me back to my apartment.

As soon as he puts me down, I eagerly open the door, flushed and panting but instantly the sound of T.V playing hits my eardrums. Frowning my confusion, I push open the door completely, hoping to find it empty but my blood runs cold and my heart drops into the pit of my stomach as I stagger into my apartment's entryway.

Of course, things just don't go my way, especially since I'm dealing with a person like Jerome.

The sight of him on my couch, beer bottle in hand and a blunt in the other is a sight I thought I was finally free from but of course, I wouldn't be able to escape him that easily. I just stand there, staring at him. I don't know what to say, what to do, or what to think. It's like I'm in a dream that's about to turn into a nightmare.

Jerome whips around with his lips twisted into a smirk, but his expression morphs into stunned shock in the instant Rafael enters behind me.

"Who's that?" Rafael's voice lowers behind me.

Jerome takes a deep inhale on the blunt in his hand, then coughs harshly, and his eyes settle back on me, "Shit, Deonne. I didn't know you were this much of a slut. Is that where you've been the whole week? Whoring yourself out!?"

"Enough, Jerome! We broke up, my romantic life is none of your concern." I say, attempting to keep my voice steady. I glance back at Rafael, and I see his brows furrow. "Rafael, I'm sorry. He's no one. Just someone I have to deal with. You should go. I'll text you."

Placing my hands on his chest, I gently nudge him to go away before Jerome could turn everything into shit. But Rafael doesn't budge, he doesn't want to leave me there with an angry Jerome.

"We've been apart for two fucking weeks and you're already with a new guy? I should have known you were nothing but a fucking ho, a bitch for the streets!" Jerome spits.

"Don't you fucking speak to her that way."

Jerome's eyes narrow at Rafael's possessive tone. He jerks his beer bottle in Rafael's face. "And just who the hell are you?"

"The person who can make your life a literal living hell if you don't get the fuck out of her house, this second," Rafael growls and Jerome steps back in surprise. His eyes widen in fear before his face contorts back into anger.

"Just get out Jerome. Please." I say.

But Jerome laughs, an ugly sound that turns me cold. "And what am I supposed to do? Huh? Where am I supposed to go? You took everything away from me. I don't have anything left...but I'm not going to let you tell me what to do, Deonne. We may not be together anymore, but I still own you."

I feel Rafael tense and I hear his warning growl but I don't risk looking at him. I don't want to cause a scene, or for there to be a fight. But I can't let Jerome get away with it. I can't let him bad mouth me like that. Especially in front of Rafael.

"That's where you're wrong, Jerome. You don't own me. You never did." I say firmly.

This time, it's Rafael that steps forward, his jaw clenched, eyes hard as flint.

"Get the hell out of her house." Rafael ices out his words. "If you don't, I'll make you." Rafael pulls me behind himself.

Jerome's gaze snaps toward the door. But then, Jerome's gaze shifts from Rafael, then back to me and I can tell that he's trying to decide something. Finally, and with an eerie calmness, he picks up his jacket and takes another long drag of the blunt.

"Fine. I wouldn't want to be anywhere near a bitch who's been fucked all over by someone else." Jerome snarls as he turns to leave.

"Goodbye, Jerome," I say, and watch him as he walks out of my door and back out of my reality. As soon as he's out, I push the door closed behind him. My heart pounds against my chest and I feel like I've just been through a hurricane. I lock the door with a heavy sigh and fall back against it.

"I'm sorry. I didn't think...I didn't know he would still be here." I say, cringing at the low sound of my voice.

Before I can say anything else, Rafael grabs me by my shoulders and pulls me into a tight hug. "You don't owe me an explanation. As far as I'm concerned, he's a dead issue." He murmurs, his voice low.

I mask my sigh of relief.

"Thank you for tonight." I choke out, my hands still shaking, and Rafael takes them into his own. "But, I think I'm going to just...get some sleep. I just, need some time." I lift one shoulder and force a smile.

"Are you sure you'll be alright?" He asks, worry and concern clear in his voice.

I can only nod. This was for the best, I can barely remember life without Jerome. Maybe this was fate telling me that this just wasn't the right time to jump into a new love–no, a fling.

Rafael gives me a searching look and I know he wants to ask but he doesn't. Instead, he kisses me, slowly, gently, and sweetly.

"I understand. Just know that I'm here if you need me." He says, and I can feel the emotion radiating off of him.

I nod and he gives me one more kiss. The kind of kiss you give when you want to say goodbye, to wish someone sweet dreams.

"Goodnight, Deonne." He says against my lips, before he silently leaves through my door.

CHAPTER NINE

I TAKE A LONG, HOT SHOWER, TRYING TO WASH AWAY JEROME'S WORDS. But they linger, like a bad dream. When I get out of the shower, I towel myself dry, and wrap the bath towel around my body.

Back in my bedroom, I slip on a robe and lay down in my own bed, but I can't sleep. Jerome's words keep echoing in my head. He has nothing left, and he had the audacity to say that it was I who took everything from him. And the way he had looked at me then...was scary.

Laying alone upon the sheets, I tell myself that I'm safe in my own home, with locks and the alarm system. But I long for Rafael's protective embrace. I want his warmth, his strength. I want his arms around me, want to feel his lips on my skin, his hands on me. I want to hear his heartbeat and feel his breath on my neck. I want his soft, sweet voice whispering in my ear.

I miss him.

I find sleep eventually, but it's fitful and restless.

I see Rafael, only he seems troubled. He's in my bedroom and it feels like an intimate moment. He walks toward me and in my dream, he looks like he wants to tell me something, but I beat him to the punch.

"I've changed my mind...I do. I want to see you again. I want to give us a chance. I want to be with you-

He smiles, but sadly. His finger holds the rest of my words at bay.

His expression suddenly hardening, he says: "Wake up, Deonne. You're in danger!"

I jolt up in bed.

I search the room with my eyes, but find that I'm truly alone. I look at the clock and realize that it's 3:00 AM. I shake my head.

"God, I wish I had Rafael here," I say aloud, and the sound of my voice startles me. I'm not sure what's come over me, but ever since Jerome showed up in my living room, I've been feeling on edge. Like something bad is going to happen.

I get out of bed and go to my window, parting the curtains slightly, I peer outside. All is quiet and still in my neighborhood. I see no sign of Jerome. I back away from the window, and sit on the edge of my bed.

I let out a sigh and reach over my bedside table, where I keep my cell phone. I debate whether or not I should call Rafael. I know he's probably sleeping, but I need to hear his voice. Just to know he's there.

But In these wee hours of the morning, my attention is captured by a noise.

Listening closely with bated breath, I wait...

There it is again.

I get up to investigate and find the source of it. I know I'm probably overreacting, but I have to be sure. I open my bedroom door a crack, and peek into the hallway. It's dark but I can see there's someone's silhouette in the corridor...

And they're heading towards my room.

I watch as the figure comes closer and closer. The moonlight from my window is my only source of light, and it illuminates the intruder.

Jerome.

I gasp and freeze when I see him, hazily wondering what he's doing here, and why he's here in the first place. But now I can see that he's walking towards my room with a knife hanging from his hand.

He's coming.

I quickly close the door, and intend to lock it shut but it bursts open again throwing me to the floor before I get the chance. Jerome comes charging in. He didn't even attempt to knock first.

I back away from him as he towers over me, stalking closer and closer.

"Jerome! What are you doing?" I demand, trying to keep my voice from quaking. I'm scared. I'm more terrified than I've ever been in my life. I can feel my heart racing in my chest, my hands are shaking and my throat is tight.

He doesn't answer me. He just stares at me, the knife in his hand, and I slowly crawl backwards, away from him.

"Jerome! I told you already: Get out!" I repeat, and try to get to my feet. He takes another step toward me and I fall to the floor.

"Jerome!" I yell again.

He grabs me and picks me up, throwing me on the bed. He climbs atop me and holds the knife up to my neck, the cold blade against my skin. He puts all his weight on me, forcing my back into the mattress.

"Get off me!" I yell and struggle underneath him. He's too strong for me, but I still try. I fight him, and he grabs my wrists in a hand and holds them down.

I'm nearly in tears. My chest is tight and I can't breathe.

"You took everything from me. Everything!" He grunts.

"And now I'm going to take everything away from you." He says, and he starts to apply pressure to the blade.

I feel a sharp pain as the blade pierces my skin, and I cry out. Jerome grins at me, and I see the madness in his eyes.

He's totally lost it.

And then, just when I think it's over, that Jerome is going to kill me, I see a blur of movement, and something swift, barrels through my room with a burst of hot wind, and tackles Jerome off of me.

It takes me a moment longer than it should have for me to recognize what it is.

It's a person.

It's Rafael.

And he looks the same, only...different.

Cowering on the bed, I take in his appearance. His hands are clawed, a pair of large dark leathery wings have sprouted from his back, and fan out behind him, a long pointed tail sways back and forth just above the floor.

I can't believe this is the same Rafael I've been falling for. It's like he's two different people.

Jerome is terrified, I can see it in his eyes. The knife drops with a clatter from his hand and he backs away from Rafael.

"You gotta be fucking kidding me!" Jerome shouts, and starts backing away towards the window, his eyes never leaving Rafael.

Rafael turns towards me, he's still handsome as ever but there's a deadly air about him now.

"Are you hurt?" He asks, his green eyes softening. His voice, that's one thing about him that didn't change. In addition to his other changes, I see that his canine teeth have lengthened to sharp points, the sight of him is terrifying.

I can only shake my head.

"Good." He says and turns slowly back to Jerome, and he bares his fangs at my ex. "And you. I told you to never come back." Rafael says, his voice is a growl.

Rafael slowly walks towards Jerome, and Jerome backs away, still staring at Rafael in utter disbelief.

"You can't be real," Jerome says, his eyes bulging, trying to blink the man out of existence.

Finally, Rafael lets out a deep breath. He seems to have calmed down but I can tell that this is just the calm before the storm.

"Deonne? Close the door."

"What? Why?" I whisper, and I can hear the fear in my own voice.

"Just do it, baby."

I probably shouldn't but I follow his order. I shut my room door.

"Wait! What the fuck is going on?" Jerome's eyes dart back and forth between me and Rafael.

"Baby?" Rafael turns to me, taking my attention off of my cowardly excuse for an ex, and completely ignoring Jerome as he gives me the sweetest smile. "Whatever you see here today, please don't hold it against me."

My mind reeling, I only gasp, "What are you talking about?"

He ignores my questions and his eyes flash red again but this time they don't return to their beautiful sea green. Now they glow blood red, the pupils within mere slits. Turning back to Jerome, he stalks towards him like an animal finding his prey.

"What the fuck are you!?" Jerome shouts in fear. His primary concern is the fallen knife, and he scrambles for it as Rafael steps forward. But before he can make another move Rafael grabs him by the throat, lifting him a few centimeters off the ground so that they're eye to eye.

Rafael speaks a language I can't decipher as Jerome's eyes widen in terror, this goes on for a long several seconds. His mouth falls open in a silent scream and he's released to drop to the ground on his knees. Rafael finishes his chant before turning back to me. The red is fully gone from his eyes and in its place is the beautiful green that I'm slowly falling in love with.

He gazes at me with a sad expression, but despite what I've just witnessed, I want nothing more than to pull him into a tight hug.

"I never wanted you to see that...or any of this." He shrugs and looks down at the floor. Slowly his wings and tail dissipate in a breath of flames, but the change in him hasn't completely faded.

"Well, what exactly am I seeing?"

With a languid gesture towards Jerome, he says: "Just keep watching. If you meant what you said, then watch and then tell me if you still want to be with me."

Turning back to Jerome, I watch as instructed, Jerome is frozen in the state where Rafael left him. On his knees, mouth agape but his eyes stare blindly ahead as if seeing something I can not.

Suddenly, his eyes roll back to the back of his head and blood drips from his lower lids, like tears down his cheeks. He shakes and convulses as his skin turns pale.

"W-what's happening to him?"

"Watch."

Soon Jerome's pallid skin darkens until it's gray, his mouth releasing a single whimper. "Please...stop."

Those are his last words before his body decays, crumbling, and cracking. Soon, nothing remains of Jerome but burnt ash on my carpet. It was almost fitting that dust was what he left behind since all he did was ash up my carpet with his cigarettes.

"What just happened? Where is he?"

"Where he belongs. Hell." Rafael answers back, gazing at the remains with a look of disgust. Turning back to me, he looks down at his feet in shame.

"And you sent him there?"

He nods his head silently.

"Will you tell me how?"

"I will, just please don't leave me after you hear everything."

CHAPTER TEN

R AFAEL GRABS MY HAND, PULLING ME CLOSER TO HIM AND I DON'T FIGHT HIM BECAUSE EVEN AFTER ALL OF THAT, I STILL TRUST HIM WITH MY LIFE. More than I've ever trusted anyone.

"Let's get out of here. If I'm going to tell you everything. I'd prefer to do it with no reminders of him."

Nodding in understanding, I move to go out of the door but he only holds me in place. With a whoosh of air, we're no longer in the apartment, instead, we stand on the balcony of his hotel room.

The moon shines full and bright but no stars can be seen in the sky.

"How the hell did we get here?"

"Magic." He answers simply, walking towards the edge. He leans against the railing, staring up at the sky.

If he had spoken to me about magic before I would have just laughed at him but after what I just watched, after what just happened to Jerome, I couldn't find it in me to even make a joke about it.

Walking towards him, I lean against the railing beside him, studying the pained look on his face. As much as I want to hear everything, I only really want to ease his pain and bring back the smile that graced his features from earlier.

"I'm not human, Deonne...I'm not pure like you."

"No one is pure, Rafael. No human is."

"But you are, Deonne. You're so pure that you're able to see the good in people even in scum like him. I don't deserve to be with you but whatever is up there likes to make jokes and decided to lump you in with me."

"What does that even mean?"

Sighing heavily, he pushes off the railing to look at me.

"I'm what your kind calls a demon. I'm an incubus to be exact. I feed on human lust. That night when you had that dream, you had just been a target." He admits with a hint of shame.

"You mean, I wasn't fantasizing about you?" I say playfully, hoping to lighten the mood. The whole idea of him being a demon is still hard to swallow.

"I'm sorry that I took advantage of you, but you were too good of a catch to just pass up." He looks at me and I'm taken aback by the wanton hunger in his eyes. "You looked like you needed it. At the time, I thought of you as just a beautiful but lonely soul with a lot of unfulfilled lust but then after that night, I couldn't feed anymore."

And when he looks at me, he seems a bit confused himself.

"Nothing, no one, can satiate me anymore. I've heard stories about it, of incubi finding what could be called a "soulmate". Someone who can fulfill the everlasting hunger that fills us. They call it our salvation but I never believed it." His eyes flash red as he stares at me intently. "Until I met you."

Grabbing my heart, he places his hand on his chest. "I've never felt something inside me until I saw you. I'm hungry for no one else but you. That's why I set up that whole mixer. Why I compelled your friend Beverly to make you go."

"So, you planned everything from the start?"

"I did. The mixer, bumping into you, your day off. Everythi ng...almost everything. I thought I could hide it from you, that other side of me, but then I saw Jerome. I could see everything he did to you and everything he wanted to. I couldn't hold myself back, I had to punish him."

"And where is he now?" I ask, not really caring about what happens to him but more out of curiosity.

"I told you. Hell. Where he belongs. From where I emerge. And where he can be played with by other beings like me. Those who like to inflict pain and feed on suffering."

He reaches out to me almost hesitantly, before letting his hand fall to his side.

"I understand if you want to go. And it's okay. I won't ever bother you again, if you do." His voice cracks, and he looks down at his feet.

Grabbing his hand in mine, I tilt his chin up with the other.

"If hell is from where you came and will return to. I'll go with you. I'll stay with you wherever you have to go. Whether that's hell or heaven or here. I just want to be by your side." I place a kiss on his lips and I hope that's enough for him to understand what I feel.

The moment I had dreamed of him, I knew that he's what I wanted, what I needed.

"If you're eternally damned to everlasting hunger, then let me be the one to satiate you. Let's be damned together."

CHAPTER ELEVEN

A T MY WORDS, RAFAEL LIFTS ME UP WRAPPING MY LEGS AROUND
HIS WAIST AS I STARE DOWN AT HIM.

"There's no going back from this. You need to be sure, because, if you say yes, I'll never let you go. I will send any other man that touches you down to Hell and spend all of my resources to search for you to the ends of the earth." He looks back at me and I can tell he means every word.

"I'd be disappointed if you didn't."

"Well, we can't let that happen then." Carrying me into the room, he throws me on the bed.

"You know, I've been holding back because I didn't want to scare you away but now that you know everything, I guess there's no need for me to hold back anymore." He strips himself completely naked before me.

His body tallens, and his muscles bulge. Wings unfurl from his back in a fiery flicker, stretching to the limits of the bed. His tail twitches behind him, its tip curling up before it wiggles teasingly. My eyes grow wide at the sight of him in his fully demonic form.

His demon side is so dominant that it's scary, but I'm not scared. I'm excited.

My eyes can't help but travel down his gorgeous body until they reached his manhood, standing strong and proud before me. It seems to be waiting, begging for me to come and play with it. To explore and indulge in its bulbous head, its pulsing veins, and to taste the salty pre-cum that's now dripping from the tip.

"Is this what you want, Deonne?" He asks huskily as he takes his cock in his hand and gives it a couple of strokes up and down. Then he brings his hand to his mouth and tastes it, closing his eyes to savor the taste.

"Yes." I breathe out but I don't move from my spot.

His eyes turn into a deep shade of red and they don't revert to their original state . His handsome features darken as he prowls towards me, and as a sultry smile curves his lips, his fangs grow long in his mouth.

"So you want to see what a demon can do, huh?" He crowds me with his body.

I don't think I can ever get tired of this sight. He calls himself a demon but all I can see now is an angel, and the best part about it is that I know for a fact that he feels the same way about me too.

"Then show me what you've got. Show me how a demon can fuck." My voice is thick with desire.

"Don't say I didn't warn you," He smirks, and starts to draw my skirt down my hips with long, slow strokes of his fingers.

Then, without so much as a warning, he tears my clothes to shreds, leaving the scraps of fabric scattered all around me. I couldn't even bring myself to care that my outfit probably cost him a fortune.

He stares back down at me and I didn't even know it was possible but his eyes turn an even darker shade of red as he stares down at my naked form.

"I love you."

His words freeze time for a minute. I've heard Jerome tell me those three little words before but it has never made me feel anything like what I'm feeling now. And I realize it must be because I never truly loved him.

He had held me hostage with my insecurities and his verbal abuse that when I was with him I had mistaken my desperation for love but now as I stare back at the man who literally is a demon in human form, whatever I felt could not compare to this.

No one has ever made me feel this good about myself and for once in my life, I feel seen. Perhaps, when he said we were soulmates, it was true. But, I'm not his salvation, he is mine. If I had never met him in my dreams, then I would have spent my whole life living in a haze that I never truly knew I was in.

Gazing back at him, I smile. "I love you too."

"I don't deserve you."

"Even if you think that way, you're the only one who can have me. Soul be damned. I don't need heaven. I just need you."

Grabbing my hands, he pins them down over my head and he leans down over me. His every touch is electric.

Covering my body with his, I feel my skin erupt in tingles, every inch of my flesh that touches his vibrates in arousal that I have never experienced before. It's like my body is on fire and yet I welcome the heat.

His tongue, long and forked, runs over my lips and I shudder at the sensation. He places his mouth on mine and kisses me roughly like any minute I'll just disappear. Wrapping my arms around his neck, I pull him closer to me.

I moan as his tongue invades my mouth, tasting and teasing me. His saliva is like a drug, sending a wave of pleasure through my body that has me arching up to meet him.

Pulling away, he plants soft kisses into my throat, and then his teeth sink into the flesh of my neck, and the sharp pain mixes with pleasure.

It's like nothing this man does can hurt me. Like he was made entirely just for my pleasure. He slides his tongue over the wound and I feel my eyes roll back into my head. It's like he's kissing my soul.

"You're mine," he growls.

"Ahhh..." I moan as I feel his the tip of his throbbing dick pulse against my core. The feeling of his cock rubbing against me is almost too much. His hands grab and squeeze two handfuls of my ass, his hips jerk forward again and again.

"Please...I want you inside me-" I barely finish gasping before he sheathes himself inside me with a single thrust, balls deep to the hilt and I scream.

"Fuck." He groans when I'm completely filled with his enormous cock, I clench around him. Thrusting his hips, his tail snakes out from behind him and wraps its way around my leg. I grab the sheets to ground myself as pain mixes with pleasure.

He wraps a hand around my throat, squeezing tightly and restricting my airflow. My moans come out as mewls, and he continues to ram his cock inside me. He works his way in and out of me in a steady rhythm and pumps until I'm nearly numb from the pleasure radiating from my core.

His movements are fast and rough, he stretches me in a way that borders on painful, that's almost too much for me. I close my eyes, letting myself be drowned in the sensations he causes. My mind is swimming in lust and my body is covered in a fine sheen of sweat.

"Look at me." He growls and my eyes snap open.

I stare at his red eyes as they swirl like orbs putting me in a lust-filled haze.

"Who do you belong to?" His voice is hypnotizingly deep and velvety.

"You." I say breathlessly. "I'm yours."

Rafael's face changes from one of lust to one of determination. Pumping into me, he grabs ahold of my legs and pulls them up to my chest, bending me nearly in half. I raise my arms over my head and grip the wooden headboard, bracing myself as he slams into me. The sound of our flesh meeting fills the room, echoing through the walls.

"I can't hear you. Who do you belong to?" His words bring me closer and closer to my orgasm. He thrusts harder into me, going deeper and reaching parts of me that I thought wasn't possible, making me impossibly wetter.

"I'm yours, Rafael!" I shout as he keeps his pace. The bed rocks from the force of movement, but we ignore it.

"Then, cum for me." He demands and that pushes me over the edge.

"Rafael, I'm cumming!" I scream, losing all control of my body. My orgasm hits me like a freight train and my muscles clench around him, until my vision turns black. I feel my body become flush and lightheaded. With one final thrust, Rafael comes with a roar, his seed filling me completely. His wings unfurl and wrap around us like a blanket.

"Fuck, Deonne!" He gasps, thrusting through his orgasm.

His rougher movements and his deep moans send me spiraling into another orgasm that keeps on coming and coming, making my muscles clench around him. His thrusts finally start to slow down and he collapses on top of me, letting go of my throat, to wrap his arms around me, squeezing me tight.

"That was amazing." I pant and he lays on top of me using my breasts as a cushion.

"You're amazing, he responds, placing a kiss on the mound of my breast.

"So what does this mean for us?" I question. "Will you take me to hell and be your demon wife where we will spawn our demon children?

He chuckles at my question, lightly biting my nipple. "If you'd have me. Although I wouldn't really recommend going down to hell it's a bit difficult to make it back here."

"Then should we just have our children here then?"

"That sounds nice."

The next morning, I woke up to the sun shining against my face. Rafael lies beside me still fast asleep but I can feel wetness dampen my panties. I had dreamed about him again.

Although, I can't really be too sure if it was just a dream or if that was Rafael doing his incubus stuff again. Shifting slightly, I run my hand through his hair and he stirs.

His eyes flutter open, and I'm greeted by the deep green eyes that I've fallen in love with.

"Good morning," he mumbles as he gives me a sweet smile. "Had a pleasurable dream?'

"Mmhm." I hum in response, playing with his soft locks as he sighs in contentment, leaning further against my touch.

"What was it about?"

"A gorgeous man, only inhuman."

"Uh-huh. And then what happened?" He asks with a smirk as his hands trail down to my pussy. I giggle, rolling my eyes, knowing all too well that he already knows what happened.

"Oh, you know. Just your average, typical *Wet Dream.*"

ABOUT THE AUTHOR

About The Author

Lexis Esme is a writer of steamy erotic romance stories featuring beautiful black heroines of every variety, and the gorgeous men (and supernatural beings) who love them. Lexis believes that everyone should be able to see themselves wined, dined, seduced, romanced, and even ravaged in their choice of romantic literature, and love interests of every variety to cherish them. Seeing a lack of the kind of main love interests that look like her, she set out to create as many of these stories as she possibly can for readers who might feel the way she does, or simply just want to see something new. Variety is the spice of life after all, and Lexis loves to keep it spicy.

Based in Canada, she spends her days walking the nearby nature trails dreaming up romantic and sexy new adventures and scenarios, the steamier the better. She also loves experimenting in the kitchen, dancing, drawing and reading. She never ever has enough books, shoes, or chocolate.

She is currently hard at work on a new series of sexy novellas and various other erotic short stories.

Be on the look out for Lexis's website, and socials coming soon!

ALSO BY LEXI ESME

THREADS OF FATE Excerpt

CHAPTER 1 – RHIANNE

I lean my head against the window of Gary's sleek black Mercedes and look at the passing scenery. It's a dark cloudy night, the windows are dotted with the beginnings of an autumnal shower, and my guilt is eating me alive.

"Looks like there's a storm coming," I say, breaking the silence.

"Yup," Gary says, he turns on the wipers, and they swipe at the sparse droplets on the windshield.

I hear the distant crack of thunder, and I quickly say, "I don't like thunderstorms."

I shift in my seat to face him. "I'm really sorry about this, Mr. Edwards," I begin. "I could've gotten a taxi or used a ride share app--you didn't have to go through the trouble-"

"Rhianne, really, it's fine. How were you to know that your car would break down outside in the parking lot?" he says. He raises his thick salt and pepper eyebrows and smiles at me.

"Yeah, but I feel so bad. We've been at work for almost ten hours, and now you have to take me home."

"Eh, what's another hour of civic duty?" he says, smirking. I sigh, and Gary pats my hand. "I'm only teasing. Really, Rhianne, it's fine. After hours, we're not just boss and employee; we're friends. Friends take care of friends. Isn't that your motto? Speaking of, I told you a hundred times to call me Gary."

"You're right. Sorry Mr.--, I mean, Gary," I quickly correct myself with a bashful smile. He laughs again, and I relax a little more in my seat.

I refocus my sights on the view outside. The city's lights slowly drown out, and all I can see are tall trees and twists of the road beyond the raindrops on the windows. The rain gets harder and harder, and the wipers struggle to keep up.

There's barely anyone else on the road, and as we continue, I notice that signage grows few and far between. I look down at my hands, folded neatly in my lap, wring them together, then give the dashboard clock another glance. It's only eight-thirty. I shouldn't feel this anxious, and yet, I do. I lick my lips and glance at Gary.

"Uh, Gary," I venture hesitantly, my voice just above the tinny pattering of rain against the car roof. Gary glances at me quickly in the rearview mirror, and then his eyes fall back on the road ahead.

"This isn't the way to my house." I go on, a little more sharply now. "Maybe you should turn on the GPS. I don't want you to get lost."

Gary snorts. "Relax. This is a shortcut. I take this way all the time to get to your home."

I furrow my brows, trying to think back to the last time I invited him over. I can't dredge up a memory of it.

"I'm sorry, when have you been to my house?"
His silence makes the short hairs on the back of my neck
stand. "When have you been to my house?" I repeat.
He only continues to stare forward. "Do you remember when
you came to *Visionaries* to work for me?" He asks offhanded-
ly, catching me off-guard. "I do. It was one of the best days
of my life. You were so impressive during your interview. I
knew I was going to hire you. And over the years, I never once
regretted the decision. Not once."
I watch as the number on the speedometer increases from
forty miles per hour to sixty. The click of the locks makes me
jump in my seat, and I suddenly feel claustrophobic. I can't
find any words to say, so I keep quiet. Gary doesn't seem to
notice, because he keeps on without pause.
"It didn't take long for me to fall madly in love with you." He
chuckled harshly. "And you *rejected* me."
"I don't date people I work with. It's a rule of mine...Besides,
you're my boss, and I'm not comfortable with that." I wonder
what happened to the traffic. I search the other lanes, but
they're empty.
"Rhianne, I never once questioned your rejection until you
flirted with me."
"I've never flirted with you." I try to keep my indignation--and
disgust--out of my tone.
He turns and faces me. The gray of his eyes is so dark they
make him look soulless. "Two years ago, April 17th, you *com-
plimented* me on my tie. Your exact words were, 'Good pick.
It goes well with your suit.' One year ago, July 24th, you called
me Gary for the first time." He closes his eyes, causing the car
to swerve slightly. "The way it rolled from your lips left me
hard all day..."
A shiver goes down my spine. I open my mouth to say something, but I'm so flabbergasted I shut it again. Did he just say
what I think he said?

"...From then on, I knew you were mine, and I always protect what is mine. I followed you home every day to make sure you were safe...and alone." His thin lips curl into a smile that makes my stomach drop. "You knew I was there. I know you did. That's why you always undress in front of the window, behind that sheer curtain. You *wanted* me to see that perfect body of yours."

His hand reaches out tremblingly before he rests it on my thigh giving it a squeeze, I jerk away from him, but he only grips tighter. "Tinkering with your car was my play in our game, but how about we skip the song and dance we've been doing for two years and get to the point? Things have gotten dicey at work, and we need to get out of town for a bit."

"I'm not going anywhere with you--" I gasp. "Don't do this. If you take me home right now, I promise all is forgiven. I won't tell anyone. We can just go back to how things were."

"But don't you get it? I want you to tell. I want you to tell the world how good I made you feel. I want you to show them you're mine." He yanks the wheel to the right, and the car careens from the road.

Slamming his foot on the brake pedal, he halts the car a mere moment before it collides into a tree. All I could hear was the sound of the rain and the beating of my own heart. In the seclusion of the woods, he unbuckles his seatbelt and faces me. Meanwhile, I pull feverishly at the door handle.

"Knock it off!" he screams, reaching for me.

I swat at his beefy hands, but he easily catches my wrist, yanking me across the seat. "Stop, Gary! Please!--" Recoiling from him, I try to twist out of his grip.

"I said fucking knock it off!" he shouts, drawing his hand back. The sting of his slap sends my head snapping to the side, and my head rings. And for a moment, everything in me is frozen, and my brain can't form a single coherent thought. I can taste the coppery tang of blood, I feel it pooling from my nose.

Tears fill my eyes, but I blink them away.

"You think you're better than me, huh? You think I don't deserve you? I *made* you. You are nothing without me. Maybe you need a reminder of that."

He unlocks the door and rushes to the passenger side before I can react, and he wrenches my door open, pulling me out by my hair into the rainy night.

I try to claw my way away from him, but he throws me onto the sodden earth. My head slams against a stone, and the world around me seems to fade.

"Rhianne?"

His words are muffled, and he swims in my vision, I can barely make out his expression.

"Rhianne?!" Gary's hands fly to his mouth, and he fumbles to find my pulse. I feel myself fading, but I fight it.

"Rhi-ahhh!--"

It takes nearly all my strength, but my foot connects squarely with his groin, and I watch him crumple over.

"You bitch!" Gary rasps, holding his crotch.

I scramble to my feet, but in my disorientation, the entire world moves in a crooked circle. I fall onto my hands and knees onto wet leaves, dirt and gravel, but I use them as leverage to push myself up to my feet once again. Thoroughly drenched and covered in dirt, I take off into the blackened woods.

"Help!" I plead as I draw further into the darkness. Leaves crunching behind me tell me Gary isn't far behind, and he laughs wildly in pursuit.

"I love this new game!"

My heart is pounding out of my chest, and my lungs burn with every breath I take, but I can't stop. My feet splashing in the puddles, I race deeper into the woods.

All at once, a flash of lightning illuminates the forest like a camera flash; the trees become stark silhouettes against a dreary sky.

"Help! Please, help!" The sound of my yelling is swallowed by the heavy rain, whipping wind, and the bone-rattling boom of thunder.

Gary's footfalls are moments away now, and I can almost feel his breath on my neck.

Please...someone...please help.

I think a silent prayer to myself, but I'm not sure to who.

Just as Gary's hand grabs a fistful of my hair, I feel my feet lose purchase of the ground beneath me, it loosens and splits, crumbling beneath my feet like it's made of sand.

Before I know it, I'm tumbling down, with Gary falling after. My heart in my throat, I scream.

My arms flail wildly as I try to find something to grab onto. But I slam into the ground hard on my back, the air driven from my lungs.

A loud bang follows, just inches from me, as Gary falls into the pit shortly after. He doesn't move.

"Gary?" I say.

No answer comes.

"Gary?" I try again.

Nothing.

Trying to adjust to the darkness, I blink several times, squeezing my eyes shut. I lift myself up from the ground as quickly as my aching body will allow. I strive to see in the pitch blackness of the place, but as the clouds shift overhead, a soft ray of moonlight allows me to make out a dirt-covered wall beside me.

I look down at myself. I'm covered in wet dirt, my clothes torn, and bloodied. My entire body aches from the fall, but I'm alive. Just as quickly the clouds converge like a curtain dropping on a stage. All is in darkness again. I can't make out most of my surroundings, but it seems, we've landed in a pit. It's relatively drier down here; the air hangs damply, heavily, and thick with the smell of earth and nitrates.

My hands grope blindly along the walls of the place to find a steady foothold, a rock, a vine, anything. My fingers soon discover something hard and curved, and I smirk imagining it to be a tree root. Grabbing hold, I test some of my weight on it, but it shifts in the dirt wall, causing me to lose balance. I stagger back, from it but my hand comes away sticky and with much effort.

Wonderingly, and still half dazed, I open and close my hand, feeling a clinging substance stretching between my fingers, like stretchy sap-covered hairs or vines. I wonder at what I just touched, I try to wipe my hand clean against my torn pencil skirt, and it very nearly adheres. I'm forced to rip my hand back, with a shuddering breath.

Something feels so wrong about this place, and I begin to wonder where I am in earnest. And as though in answer, there is a sudden and momentary flash of lightning. I can make out the walls that surround me, and ice pours through my veins.

"Oh my God."

The pit extends far beyond, and behind me and Gary, far above us too, but what lines the pit is truly horrifying: Shredded clothing. Bones. Disturbingly familiar-looking shapes, swathed, cocooned, in thick layers of a fine white fabric substance. And lacing the walls, miles of silvery threads.

Spiderwebs?

Recognizing the impossible material, I want to scream. Nothing comes out.

Worse still, a sound carries in the darkness just a few short feet away.

"Fuck..."

It's almost a relief to hear that it's only Gary. I can just barely make him out, struggling to sit up.

He groans in pain. Finally, having come to, I see his silhouette rise to his feet. I hear a jingling of car keys before a thin beam of yellow light cuts through the darkness. For an instant, I'm grateful Gary is here until I remember he just assaulted me and likely has plans for worse.

I step back away from the light, my hands raised to shield my eyes.

"Rhianne?...Well, at the very least, I still have you here with me...it looks like I haven't lost everything. I would have taken you with me, Rhianne, we could've lived a beautiful life together, but you don't seem to want that, which means I'll have no use for you after tonight. At the very least, this is the perfect place to leave you to rot if you continue to disrespect me."

Damn it. I guess not even circumstances can change Gary's priorities.

I retreat a half-step from him before he redirects the beam of light elsewhere. He shines the mini flashlight along the walls, lingering on what I've witnessed, but not quite understanding what he sees. I can see it in the faint light; his hand is shaking.

"Where am-"

But his sentence breaks as yet another noise whispers through the darkness, a faint crackling. Following the sound with his flashlight, the beam lands at a far corner, where something shadowy quickly slips from view.

"Christ!" The flashlight drops from his hands, made clumsy in his fear. Keys and all fall to the ground in a cacophony of jingling; and all is lost to darkness once again.

"What was that?" I whisper in a harsh breath. Wondering if I'd seen anything at all.

"Shit...shit." Is all Gary says, fumbling around for his keys.

And then we both see it. Red eyes peer back at us from the abyssal dark, and contortions of bone fill the night air.

Gary stumbles backward, and keen, rubied eyes follow his every movement.

The next part happens in slow motion, as though in a nightmare.

I watch as an enormous thin pointed appendage amasses from the darkness. Black and lacquered, reflecting the faintest moonlight, it plants itself firmly in the earth.

I hear Gary staggering back, his heel accidentally kicking the car keys; they bounce off into the darkness, lost.

Several uneven shafts of moonlight reveal the scene unfold before me. Gary's eyes bulge at the sight of the other. He can't speak. He can only watch as the creature reveals more of itself. The sight of another leg, and then another, make his face lose all color. He turns and locks eyes with me, the fear on his face making my own double.

He opens his mouth, but no words rise from his throat. Instead, a loud gargle pierces the silence. I feel a scattered spatter of warm liquid across my face and clothing, and I damn near hyperventilate.

Shakingly, Gary looks down at his chest. Velvet blood pools and stains the ground as the creature's leg twists inside of him.

It pulls Gary from his feet and several feet into the air.

Blood pours from his open mouth, and he wraps his fists around the wrist-thick appendage that holds him impaled and suspended, to no avail. His grip slips off the creature like it's coated in oil.

"H-help me," he chokes out to me, but I can only sink to my knees, my legs having lost all feeling.

Gary is easily pulled towards the creature, toward the dark body that seems to absorb all of the light. It lashes band after band of silk webbing around him, the shiny threads glistening like silver stripes in the otherwise steady tapestry of shadows and darkness. Gary's legs kick spastically in the air, but hauntingly, I watch as the creature runs another dark appendage down Gary's horrified face in a final caress.

It's almost calm, deep growl comes back to me: "Hush, be silent now."

I look on, horrified.

It lifts him higher, twining the fine threads around and around his legs, working quickly to cocoon him compactly, like its victims in the walls. And sickeningly, I hear hollow cracking sounds, like a branch snapping in half, as the creature twists and pulls, and tightens, seemingly only finding the fruitless struggles of its food amusing. The flailing Gary screams as bones are broken, but the sound is soon choked back down his throat. Gary's screams are silenced in a moment. The creature quickly wraps the last of the silky substance over his head then continues to envelop him until he is silent, until he is still. Gary's tightly cocooned form is hoisted on a silken rope, slung up, and secured in a high corner.

I feel sick as my gaze lowers to my hand, covered in the unknown substance, now also dotted with blood, realizing it is the very same substance Gary is enshrouded in. I can't get the image of Gary's face, his cries, the sound of his breaking bones, out of my head.

I can hear the creature approaching, its slow and heavy footfalls sounding out as it turns, like it's looking to me, as though noticing me for the first time.

In a blind panic, I turn away from the horror of the creature and begin to crawl on all fours. I don't see a way out, and I don't know where I am going, I just go.

Time slows.

I don't want to look up and face the creature that I know scales the walls above me. Quaking, I lift my head, my scream is amplified by the walls around me as it lunges directly at me.

CHAPTER 2 – RHIANNE

Encased in the darkness, I shut my eyes tightly and hear the heavy thud of the creature land in front of me. I wait for the singe of its fangs, or the pierce of its leg to sink into my flesh as it did Gary. I cringe against the cool bare earth of the pit.

"You shouldn't be here..."

He? It definitely sounds like a he, speaks again, and there's something almost elegant in his voice, a slight accent I cannot place.

No--fucking--duh I shouldn't be here.

I'm so terrified my voice won't come at all, but I manage: "Let me go, please..." I can't hold back the shudder as my words finally break free from my lips.

The creature doesn't answer for a time. Finally, it responds: "What is your name?"

I raise my head but can't make myself open my eyes to face the enormous monster in front of me.

I open my mouth to answer, but the only thing that comes out is a choked sob. Trying again, I stammer: "R-Rhianne...please, I--"

The creature doesn't even allow me the chance to beg for my life, it simply says back, voice soft: "Rhianne? A pretty name." My name sounds almost like a caress on its lips, and it is silent once again.

For a pretty meal, I suppose.

I don't dare voice the thought aloud, I don't say anything. It takes a step closer and my lungs seize, my thoughts scatter like leaves in a storm. I can only kneel in fear. I can feel it towering over me, so much so that I am forced to squeeze my eyes shut and face my knees.

"Are you going to eat--?" I can't bare to finish the sentence. My breath rushes out in a silent scream as I hear the creature's leg jab into the ground next to me and draw nearer.

"Should I eat you?" He sounds almost amused.

I shake my head desperately. "But, you're a monster--and I thought-"

A deep exhale comes from up above me, and I open my eyes. It's still too dark to make out his features, silhouetted and still mostly lost to shadow. I can only see that he towers above me (whether I'm sitting or standing), his hulking body, and spider-like appendages surrounding me like a cage.

"A monster..." He chuckles, and the sound is hollow. I detect something thoughtful, but also sad in his tone and guilt hits me instantly. "It is not the first time I've been given that name. I have no plans to harm you. Interestingly enough, from your screams earlier, I doubt I am the only monster you've encountered tonight."

My eyes travel to the dark wet patch of dirt where the earth has drunk deep of Gary's blood. Did he think he had saved me? Then again, I suppose he has.

"D-Do *you* have a name?" I ask, now unsure of what to say.

"Me?" His tone is almost one of surprise, and I hear the low rumble of laughter. "I suppose I have many names, among them 'Monster'."

"I'm sorry--I shouldn't have said that--" My face burns with chagrin, but then I wonder why I should feel this way at all.

"No need to be...I don't blame you, under these circumstances and most any other, to you I would seem quite...monstrous."

He pauses. "I am called Sephtis..."

"Sephtis?" I repeat, from far above me I sense he gives a nod, the faintly red glow of his eyes dances. I then realize how utterly stupid it is of me to be doing this. I'm talking to a giant, man-eating spider-being in a pit, with absolutely no means of escape.

He claims he doesn't plan to hurt me. I reason. *Gary claimed to want to help me...he didn't have the intention of hurting me either. Until he did, and planned on hurting me far worse...*

"If we are done with the pleasantries, I would like for you to leave, Rhianne." The leg that had stabbed the ground beside me, slowly rises before my face and I flinch back, only to realize, that Gary's keys now hang from its sharp-clawed end, flashing silver in the moonlight. He's offering it to me.

"Oh." I cup my hands together, and with a resonant jingle, he drops the damp, cold key ring into my palms.

I peer up at the hole that I'd fallen through. The trees above stand hunched over the opening, releasing their rainwater from their overhanging knobby branches and exposed roots in a steady drip.

A ray of moonlight shows me how far I'd really dropped. Tens and tens of feet, it's a wonder I didn't break anything.

"I can't get out of here," I say softly. My eyes widen in the dark when his silhouetted form bends into a bowed position from high above.

"Then, I'll take you," he says gently. I remain rooted to the ground. The broken bones, and cocoons of the dead surrounding me are seared in my mind, and knowing he was the one responsible makes it almost too unbearable to look at him, to be so close. I feel sick.

"I have told you already that I have no interest in eating you. I have no desire of anything from you, but for you to leave...as quickly as possible. If you wish the same, you have no choice but to trust me." He remains bowed, waiting for my approach.

This was true. If he wanted to devour me, he could've made quick work of me like he had Gary.

Reaching through the darkness, my hand grazes something long and silky, but not sticky.

Is this hair?

I grip onto it, and he lets out something like a muffled hiss. I yank my hands back in apology, "Sorry!" I say, self-consciously.

I tentatively reach out to him again, and I feel him lower himself to my level. My fingers glide across smooth bare skin; it's hot but not scalding, his warmth is somehow reassuring. At my touch, I hear him deepen a breath that he'd been holding. I feel the gentle rise of a heaving chest, its firm give beneath my fingertips, then the deep ripple of abs... my hands trace his shape, following crisp angles of defined musculature. This close, there is no missing the sheer size of him. Standing before me he's taller than any man has the right to be, given his long spider-like appendages.

But on top, he feels human...what the hell?

Sephtis snatches my hand, halting my investigation. "Please, take my hand," I hear him say tightly. I can tell he's trying not to sound impatient, but it's slightly condescending.

I grip his strong, much-too-human hand and I feel myself hauled from the ground and just about thrown over his shoulder onto his back. And now the differences are made much more clear. His top half is almost identical to that of a man, is that of a man's, but his bottom half is where I really see--and feel it.

It's spider-like in every way, with a hard thorax, a bulbous abdomen, and eight thick, long, spidery legs that held him in the air, just as he was. This part of him is covered in what I can only guess is a hard smooth exoskeleton, as dark as the deepest shadows. The overall effect is unsettling, but also strangely intriguing in a twisted sort of way.

I feel my own heart quicken as he begins to move, and I clutch him around the waist to keep from losing my balance. I feel his muscles tighten beneath my grip, and he quickens his pace. "Hold on tightly," His voice is still calm, but now it has an edge. We rise and fall across the uneven ground, until he begins at a steep vertical incline, and begins to scale the dirt walls of the pit, and I feel my stomach drop. My grip tightens, I keep my head down my face buried in his slick black hair that flows curtain-like down his back. His scent is earthy and rich, a strange mix of woody and spice I can't quite put my finger on. It's a pleasantly dizzying aroma.

We're moving exceptionally fast, and the light of the night sky increases, revealing the pale skin of his shoulders, veined with what looks to be thin black markings and of which I realize, there are four. And four arms. Two upper and two lower. As he scales the wall, he brushes aside debris and broken tree limbs with his hands. I try to get a view of his face, but the sharp line of his jaw is all that's visible to me from this angle.

Almost reaching the top, he jerks to a halt. "You will have to go the rest of the way alone," he says. "I cannot leave here."

"But, why?" I breathe before I can stop myself.

"That...is none of your concern." He says, and there's a sharpness to his tone. "Grab the root, and climb up. I've taken you as far as I will go."

Sephtis's movements are quick, as he points to a hanging root above me. Despite his proximity I still can't get a clear look at him, and my curiosity burns. Despite it, I release him and grip onto the root above me. The earth loosens slightly, and I wonder if it will hold.

"It will hold." He assures me as though having read my mind. Anchoring myself, I feel strangely reluctant to leave him--he feels much more sturdy than these flimsy roots. He makes the decision for me when he carefully lowers himself beneath me and leaves me to dangle from the hanging tendrils. After a moment of probing, I find a foothold and secure myself there. I quickly glance down, but it's only to glimpse the head of dark sleek hair sink further from sight, receding back into the deep recesses and shadows of the crevasse below.

I climb up until Sephtis is far in the distance. Pulling myself up, I just manage to shimmy over the edge and roll onto my back. Finally, I draw in a massive breath of relief. I can almost hear the quiet slink of him below, then again, he could be long gone already.

I sit up, and peer over the ledge into the vast darkness below, and call out to him all the same:

"I'm sorry you can't leave!" I say, "No one should have to be alone."

No answer comes back, there is only the silence of the abyss. I pause and bite the side of my lip. "And thank you for, in your own way, saving me..."

To be continued...

Read the rest of this steamy romance by purchasing

Printed in the USA
CPSIA information can be obtained
at www.ICGtesting.com
LVHW011143010524
778880LV00012B/560

9 781990 479359